Doll Hospital™

Danielle's Dollhouse Wish

♥ ♥ ♥ ♥ ♥

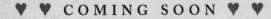

Doll Hospital™

Danielle's Dollhouse Wish

♥ ♥ ♥ ♥ ♥

BY JOAN HOLUB

Illustrations by Ann Iosa

Cover illustration by Joan Holub

A LITTLE APPLE PAPERBACK

SCHOLASTIC INC.

New York Toronto London Auckland Sydney
Mexico City New Delhi Hong Kong Buenos Aires

ISBN 0-439-40182-8

Design by Steve Scott

12 11 10 9 8 7 6 5 4 3 2 1   3 4 5 6 7 8/0
40

Printed in the U.S.A.
First printing, October 2003

For Joy Peskin,
who thought of doll hospitals.

With thanks to
my mom, Julie Hannah,
for taking me and my doll Annie to a doll hospital.

Merci beaucoup
to other friends and family who helped:
Emily, Ellen, and Lorie Ann Grover;
Sue Ford; Emily Williams; Barbara Eppenger;
George Hallowell; Cathy Williams; Patty Donna.

— J. H.

Table of Contents

Doll Hospital™

Danielle's Dollhouse Wish

CHAPTER 1

Shadows

♥ ♥ ♥ ♥ ♥

Hold still," Rose warned Bart. "Or you're going to have a weird-looking nose."

She held a big piece of black paper against the wall of her fourth-grade classroom. Bart sat in a chair between the overhead projector and her. Light from the projector made his shadow on the paper. Rose traced the outline of his head with white chalk.

Bart wiggled. "What's taking so long?" he asked.

Rose sighed. She had wanted Nadia for her partner. But their teacher, Ms. Bean, had put her with Bart instead. Now he was driving her crazy.

"Don't you want your silhouette to look good for Open House?" she asked.

"It's not called Open House. It's Parents' Night," said Bart.

"Same thing. It's when parents come to check out our classroom. We called it Open House at my old school," said Rose.

All the kids in Ms. Bean's class were making a silhouette for the Which Star Am I? display. On Parents' Night, parents were supposed to guess which silhouette was their kid.

Rose drew a jagged chalk outline around the shadow of Bart's spiky hair. She didn't think his parents would have any trouble picking him out.

"Okay. Done," she said at last.

Bart came over to see the life-size silhouette of his head Rose had drawn. "Wow! I look dangerous!"

Ever since he had watched the new Danger Ranger movie, *dangerous* was his favorite word.

Rose grinned as she handed him his silhouette. "Here. Go staple your head to the bulletin board."

Bart put his silhouette aside and got another piece of black paper. "In a minute. I have to draw you first."

"Oh, right," said Rose. She sat in the chair where Bart had been. He held the new sheet of black paper on the wall so her shadow fell on it.

The overhead projector light was bright on the left side of Rose's face. She sat straight and didn't wiggle. She hoped Bart would learn something from her.

Suddenly, she heard some kids giggle. What were they laughing at? Without moving her head, Rose slid her eyes toward the left to see what Bart was up to.

There were rabbit ears on top of her head's shadow.

"Stop doing shadow puppets on my silhouette," she told Bart.

"Whatever you say, Ranger Rose," said Bart.

A second later, Rose heard more giggles. She looked to the left again. Now there was a shadow hand with a shadow finger picking her shadow nose.

She turned around and gave The Eye to Bart. "Do it right, or I'm telling Ms. Bean."

Bart grinned, showing his new braces with their lime-green rubber bands. "Okay, okay. Don't get dangerous."

Rose sat straight again, and Bart got to work drawing her.

When he finished, they both cut out their silhouettes. Bart stapled his to one of the big gold stars Ms. Bean had put on the bulletin board.

Rose lay hers on different stars, looking for the best spot.

Bart sighed. "Just pick one!"

Rose tried out a few more stars, and then finally stapled her silhouette on one of them. She stood back to look.

"Hmm. Maybe it would be better up higher," she said. "What do you think?"

"I think I'm changing your name from Ranger Rose to Ree-ah-Ranger Rose," said Bart.

CHAPTER 2
Dangerous

♥ ♥ ♥ ♥ ♥

W"e need to do our Where People Live project," Rose reminded Bart on the way back to their desks.

Bart's desk was across from hers. Emma's was next to his. Nadia sat next to Rose. The sign hanging above their four pushed-together desks said THE DREAM TEAM. There were five other teams in the class.

"Chill out," said Bart. "Parents' Night isn't till Friday. We still have a whole week."

Rose looked over at the Red Dragons team. Their projects were finished and sitting on the shelf behind them.

"We're already behind the Dragons," said Rose. "When can you come over so we can start our project?"

Just then, Nadia and Emma got back to their desks after making their silhouettes. They overheard.

"You haven't started your Where People Live project yet?" Nadia asked Rose in surprise. "You usually finish your work before everybody."

"That's when I'm working alone," said Rose. Bart was slowing her down.

"What's the hurry?" Bart asked.

"Waiting till the last minute is dangerous," said Rose.

"Yeah!" said Bart, punching a fist in the air. "And Danger is my middle name."

Rose groaned. "What are you guys building?" she asked Nadia and Emma.

"An Iroquois longhouse," said Nadia.

"We're using real branches — not craft sticks," added Emma.

"It took us a long time to find straight ones," said Nadia. "What are you making?"

"An igloo," said Rose.

"A teepee," Bart said at the same time.

Nadia looked nervous. "You haven't decided what you're building yet?"

"It's Monday, and each team has to have two projects done by this Friday!" warned Emma.

Even though Rose was worried, she didn't let on. "No problem. Our project will be done in time for Open House."

"For *what*?" asked Bart.

Rose gritted her teeth. "I mean for Parents' Night."

But she didn't want to call it Parents' Night. Because she and her little sister, Lila, didn't have any parents to bring.

CHAPTER 3
Surprise Delivery

♥ ♥ ♥ ♥ ♥

Pretend you're Far Nana," Lila told Rose as they walked home from school.

"Why?" asked Rose.

Far Nana was the nickname they'd given their grandmother five years ago, when Rose was five and Lila was three. It was because she lived far away from their apartment back in the city.

Now Rose and Lila were living with her while their parents were in Africa. Their mom and dad were doctors. The African villages where they were working weren't safe enough for Rose and Lila. So the girls had to stay behind with Far Nana.

"I have to introduce her to my teacher on Parents' Night," said Lila. "We're supposed to practice."

"Okay." Rose jiggled her heart-shaped locket, since Far Nana always jiggled her bead necklaces. Then she made pretend eyeglasses by curling her thumbs and first fingers. She held them up to her eyes and looked over the tops of them at Lila.

"Have you done your homework?" she asked, in a bossy, grown-up voice.

Lila didn't answer. She looked to the side and began speaking to the air. "Mr. Yi, may I present my grand-mother?"

Rose looked around. "Who are you talking to?" she asked.

"My teacher. I'm pretending that I'm introducing Far Nana to him," explained Lila. "Now I'll do it the other way around."

"Far Nana, may I present my teacher, Mr. Yi?" Lila asked Rose politely.

Rose switched back to her Far Nana voice. "How do you do?" she asked.

Then she dropped her finger-glasses. "You've got it down," she said, speaking in her normal voice again.

"I know," said Lila. "But all the kids are going to do it the same way. I wish I could make my Parents' Night introduction different."

"Do you know anybody else who's bringing a grand-mother instead of parents?" Rose asked Lila.

"No," said Lila.

"Then you'll be different. We both will," said Rose. "Whether we like it or not."

"Hey," said Lila, pointing ahead. "What's that?"

Rose looked.

A large wooden crate sat on Far Nana's porch. A delivery truck was parked on the street by the curb.

"Maybe it's a present from Mom and Dad!" Lila took off, running.

Rose followed, her long blond hair flying behind her. The key-chain charms dangling from her backpack clicked together.

They ran past three driveways to Far Nana's house and then up the front steps.

Rose and Lila walked around the crate on the porch, studying it from all sides.

"I bet it's a computer!" guessed Lila.

Rose shook her head. "No. It's too tall."

"A refrigerator?" asked Lila.

"Too short," said Rose. She read the mailing label. "It's from a dollhouse museum in Washington, D.C."

"It's a dollhouse? Cool!" said Lila. Her beagle backpack bounced against her as she hopped with excitement.

Far Nana came out of the house. The beads around her neck rattled, and the fringe on her macramé vest swung with each step. "Stand aside, girls. Coming through," she told them.

Behind her, a deliveryman wheeled a cart out the front door. He nodded hello to Rose and Lila. Then he expertly scooted the crate onto his cart and rolled it inside the house.

The cart bumped upstairs as he pulled it behind him, one stair at a time. Far Nana guided him into a turreted room on the third floor. Rose and Lila followed. The man went in and set the crate on the floor.

"I need to get something to open that. Be right back," Far Nana said.

"Okay," the man mumbled. He was staring around, looking confused.

The room they were in was nicknamed the witch's hat because of its tall, pointed roof. It was full of things for repairing dolls. Colorful spools of thread, fabric, and ribbons sat on shelves and hung out of drawers. And there were boxes and bags of doll parts, like eyeballs, shoes, and wigs.

"Weird stuff in here, huh?" Lila asked the delivery guy.

"You can say that again," he said.

"Weird stuff in —" Lila repeated.

Rose elbowed her. "This is our grandmother's doll hospital," she told him.

"She's a doctor," Lila added. "Our mom and dad are, too. Only our parents fix people, and our grandmother fixes dolls."

The deliveryman patted the tall crate, smiling. "Whoa. Must be a mighty big doll you've got in here."

He wheeled his empty cart out the door before the girls could explain.

CHAPTER 4
Unpacking

♥ ♥ ♥ ♥ ♥

When Far Nana came back, she had a metal crow-bar in one hand.

"Is there really a dollhouse in this box?" asked Rose.

"Should be. That's what I was expecting the museum to send," said Far Nana.

"Can we open it?" asked Lila.

"That's the plan," said Far Nana. She wedged the crowbar under the crate's lid. When the lid popped up, she slid it off.

Far Nana and Rose looked in the top.

Lila stretched on tiptoe, but she was too short to see inside. "What does it look like?"

"Just plastic wrap so far," said Rose.

Far Nana pried more boards away. Soon the dollhouse was uncrated. After the last piece of protective plastic came off, Rose and Lila finally saw what was inside.

The painted wooden dollhouse was four stories tall. Dainty lace curtains hung in each window. Two matching pots of pink flowers sat on either side of the steps leading to the double front doors.

"Far-out, isn't it?" their grandmother asked with a wide smile.

"Does 'far-out' mean 'cool' in hippie talk?" asked Lila.

"It does indeed," said Far Nana.

"Then, yes," said Lila. "This is one of the coolest things you've ever gotten to fix." She walked around the house on her knees, looking it over.

"It's beautiful," said Rose. "What's wrong with it, anyway?"

"It needs repair here and there," said Far Nana.

The girls took a closer look and began to notice some damage.

Many of the roof's shingles were cracked or missing. One corner of the house was dented, as though it had been dropped. The railing on the front steps was broken, and the paint on the outside walls was worn off in places.

Rose pointed to a sign over the front doors of the dollhouse. It read LA MAISON DE POUPÉE. "What does that say?"

Lila read it aloud. "Lay Mason dee Poopy."

Far Nana laughed. "It's pronounced *Lah May-ZOHN duh Poo-PAY*. That's French for the house of dolls. Or dollhouse."

"So it's from France?" asked Rose.

"The letter I got from the museum last week said the house was made in Paris in 1889," said Far Nana. "It was recently found in the attic of an old French boarding school, and the museum bought it."

She cleared space on her worktable, and they all helped lift the dollhouse onto the table.

Rose and Lila tried to see in through its small windows.

"It's dark in there," Lila complained. "I can't see anything."

"How does it open?" asked Rose.

"The front panel comes off," said Far Nana.

She poked a screwdriver in the slit where the front of the house fit against the side. She wiggled the tool back and forth until the front wall of the house pulled forward. Then she removed it and set it on the floor.

Lila and Rose looked in the dollhouse's rooms. Some were as big as shoe boxes. Others were as small as juice boxes.

"There are ten rooms," Lila counted.

"There are more in the attic," said Far Nana. "Two servants' bedrooms and a linen closet." She lifted the roof back on its hinges to show them three little rooms underneath it.

"Cool," said Lila.

Most of the walls were covered with wallpaper, but some were painted. There were fireplaces and chandeliers but nothing else.

"Where's all the stuff like beds and tables and chairs?" asked Lila.

"The furniture is in the other crate," said Far Nana. She picked up her notebook and started writing.

Rose could tell she was already thinking up ways to fix the dollhouse. "What other crate?" she asked.

Without glancing up from her notes, Far Nana mumbled, "The one behind the door. The delivery fellow brought it in before you got here."

Rose and Lila rushed to look. Behind the door of the witch's hat, they found a TV-size box.

Far Nana followed with the crowbar and pried open the small crate's lid.

"Yay!" Lila said, bouncing happily when she saw the little packages inside.

"Can we open them?" asked Rose.

"That would be a big help. All those little pieces take a long time to unwrap," said Far Nana. "They're delicate, so be careful. Put everything you unpack on the shelves I've cleared along the wall."

"We will," the girls promised at the same time.

CHAPTER 5
Furniture

♥ ♥ ♥ ♥ ♥

Before Rose and Lila could begin unwrapping, Far Nana's three gray cats, John, Paul, and George, began sniffing around the crate.

"Shoo," Rose said, waving a hand at them.

The cats didn't shoo.

"You'd better put them outside for a while," said Far Nana.

"Good idea," said Lila. "They might chew on the furniture."

Rose carried two cats downstairs, and Lila carried one. When Lila opened the front door, the three cats dashed out to play in the yard.

Once they were back upstairs, Rose looked around for Far Nana's fourth cat, the only black one. "Where's Ringo?"

"I don't know," said Lila. She had already unwrapped two pieces of doll furniture. "Look at these! A little piano and a cracked mirror."

Rose sat next to the crate and pulled one of the plastic-wrapped things from inside it.

They both unwrapped chairs, tables, pictures, and dishes, showing each other what they discovered.

"Tiny books!" said Rose. "They really open. And they have stories written inside!"

"Ooh! A canopy bed," said Lila.

Rose looked over. "I love those."

Lila wiggled one of the bed's legs. "It's a little wobbly."

"This bathtub is chipped," said Rose. "And the drawer in this dresser is missing a handle."

"Most of the furniture isn't broken, though. Just dirty," said Lila.

At the bottom of the crate, they found a red velvet box. A gold rope with tassels on each end was tied in a bow around it.

Rose untied it.

Lila scooted over to watch as Rose lifted the lid.

The things inside the velvet box were wrapped in white tissue paper. They were about as big as saltshakers.

"What are they?" wondered Lila.

"Extra-special furniture?" Rose guessed.

They each took one out and carefully unwrapped it.

Lila finished first. "A little girl doll!" She held it up so Rose could see.

The doll was about four inches tall and wore a long

red dress, black stockings, and red slippers. A straw bonnet decorated with flowers sat atop its wavy brown hair.

"Mine's a woman," said Rose. She showed Lila the doll she'd unwrapped. It was about six inches tall and wore a sea-green silk dress edged with lace. Its hair was twisted into a bun held in place with a jeweled comb.

"Yours must be the mother doll," said Lila.

"Rose! Lila!" called Far Nana. "Come look!"

The girls stood and went over to Far Nana's work-table. Now every chandelier and fireplace inside the dollhouse glowed with golden light.

"The house is wired for electricity," said Far Nana.

"It's so pretty!" said Rose. "Magical almost."

"It's even cooler than before," said Lila.

"Speaking of cool — look what we found," added Rose.

They showed her the two dolls.

Suddenly, there was a scratching noise behind them. They turned around and saw something black and furry digging in the tissue-filled red velvet box.

"Ringo!" they all shouted. Rose and Lila chased the black cat into the hall. He zoomed downstairs with a piece of stolen tissue paper in his mouth. A long white strip of it sailed out behind him like a kite tail.

"Bad cat," muttered Rose. She shut the door to the doll hospital so Ringo couldn't get back in.

"He loves to play with paper," said Lila. "Remember the time he unrolled the toilet paper in our bathroom?"

"Yeah," said Rose. "How could I forget?" Quickly, she checked the contents of the velvet box. "Good, it doesn't look like he messed anything up."

Together, she and Lila finished unwrapping the dolls. There were eight in all. They found a baby doll wrapped in a yellow blanket and a father doll with a black mustache. There was a butler wearing a black-and-white uniform, a maid in a blue dress covered by a white apron, a gray poodle missing an ear, and a yellow tabby cat with a broken tail.

When they finished unpacking, Far Nana smiled. She was always happy when she had dolls to fix. "This is going to be quite a job. Several of the dolls are chipped. And some of the furniture is broken."

"How long will it take to do everything?" asked Rose.

"The museum needs it all back in a week," said Far Nana.

Rose and Lila gasped.

Far Nana shrugged. "I'll have to work hard to finish in time. But first things first. Let's make supper. How about zesty zucchini fettuccini with soybean soup and carob-chip muffins for dessert?"

Rose and Lila groaned, and they all headed downstairs.

CHAPTER 6
Which One?

♥ ♥ ♥ ♥ ♥

A few hours later, Far Nana, Rose, and Lila gathered in the doll hospital again. They studied the eight little dolls on the worktable, one by one.

"Which doll should tell the story?" asked Far Nana.

Rose and Lila knew what she meant. After they'd come to live with her, they had discovered something amazing. Far Nana could talk to dolls! She could hear dolls' thoughts and tell their stories. At first, Rose and Lila hadn't believed it. But by now they were sure it was true.

"Not the baby or the dad. Or the cat or dog," decided Rose. She moved those four dolls away, leaving the mom, girl, maid, and butler.

"Not the maid or butler," said Lila. She moved them away. That left the mother doll and the girl doll.

"I vote for the little girl," said Rose

"Me, too," said Lila.

"Sounds good," said Far Nana.

Lila turned off the overhead lights in the witch's hat.

The tiny golden bulbs in the dollhouse still glowed softly like a cozy campfire.

Rose put a velvet sofa in a dollhouse room that had cream-colored wallpaper. She set the girl doll on it.

Then they pulled three chairs close to the worktable and sat down to wait. For a few minutes, the only sound was the hum of the dollhouse lights.

Finally, Far Nana spoke. And the little girl doll's story began.

CHAPTER 7
Waking Up
Danielle's Story

♥ ♥ ♥ ♥ ♥

Bonjour! Je m'appelle Danielle. J'habite dans la maison de poupée.

Oh! Pardonnez-moi. I am in America. I shall speak English instead of French, yes?

Hello! My name is Danielle. I live in the dollhouse. Did you know it was built the same year as the famous French Eiffel Tower, 1889? Both were built for a celebration called the Universal Exposition.

Eight china dolls were made for the dollhouse. There was baby Henri, Maman, and Papa. There was also our maid, our butler, our tabby cat, and our poodle. And, of course, me!

Ooh-la-la! It is good to be back in the dollhouse at last! I have been packed away for so long.

But I shall start my tale at the most important time, no? Back in 1890, after our dollhouse was given to the Boarding School for Young Ladies in Paris, France.

CHAPTER 8
Guests
Danielle's Story

♥ ♥ ♥ ♥ ♥

Our dollhouse sat on a low cabinet in the grand parlor of the school, facing the front hallway and stairs. The back of our house looked toward one of the school's large windows.

One spring day, I watched the birds peck at the fruit on the lime trees outside. When they flew away, I wished I could fly with them.

Instead, I had to stay in my chair at the table in the dollhouse dining room with Maman and Papa. Our maid and butler were serving dinner. My baby brother, Henri, was asleep upstairs in the dollhouse nursery. My cat, Mimi, and dog, Fifi, played beneath the table at our feet.

We had been at dinner for nearly two weeks. And we were all quite ready for the meal to end.

I am so bored, I said. *This is the longest dinner in history. When can I go to the dollhouse playroom?*

We must wait, Danielle, Maman told me. *You know none of us can go on our own. We need a real girl to take us.*

But none of the schoolgirls have come to play with us for so long, I said. *They are busy with their lessons.*

She's right. And I have work to do in the dollhouse kitchen, said the maid.

Well, I had to leave my new book, The Adventures of Tom Sawyer, *at a very exciting part,* said Papa. *I hope it is still on my parlor chair, awaiting my return.*

I would like to continue working on my embroidery in the dollhouse parlor, said Maman. *But there is no sense in wishing.*

Someone is coming, our butler said in his starchy voice. He was always the first to announce visitors arriving at the school's door.

It is probably just a delivery of some sort, said the maid.

No. They are coming to the front door, said the butler. *The school's doorbell will ring in a moment.*

How exciting! I said. *Only important visitors come to the front door. Milk and bread deliveries always go to the back.*

When the doorbell rang a moment later, we heard the soft pad of the schoolgirls' slippers as they scurried downstairs.

I saw them gather behind the railing on the second-floor steps. Their long, colorful skirts looked like a large patchwork quilt as they sat shoulder to shoulder. From there, they would be able to see who had come without appearing to be nosy.

There were ten girls at the small, private school. All were from wealthy families. A bossy girl named Sophie was the oldest, at age eleven.

Here comes the mistress, announced our butler.

The mistress of the school hurried into the front hallway. She straightened her gray bun and put on a smile. Then she turned the doorknob.

The door burst open. A woman with a beaklike nose pushed past her and marched inside. She tapped the silver tip of her ruffled umbrella on the marble floor with every other step.

The schoolmistress curtseyed. "Bonjour, Madame!"

"You greet your own guests? Where is your butler?" the lady demanded. "What sort of establishment is this, anyway?" She looked around the hallway and sniffed her beaky nose haughtily.

That lady looks like she smells a skunk! I said.

Oui. But it's her manners that smell, said our maid.

I giggled.

Her orange silk dress and ostrich-feather hat must have cost quite a bit, said the butler. *She's a grand lady, no doubt.*

She looks like a large, feathered pumpkin, I said. *So I shall call her Madame Pumpkin.*

Papa's mustache twitched as he snorted. It was the sound he made when he was trying not to laugh.

Don't be unkind, Danielle, said Maman.

"We don't receive many guests," the schoolmistress finally replied. "So a butler isn't —"

"Never mind!" Madame Pumpkin interrupted. "I have brought Evette to enroll in your school. For now, at least."

She turned to speak to someone behind her. "Come along, girl! Get inside," she scolded. She rapped her umbrella's tip impatiently on the floor.

Who is it? Who else has come? I wondered, bubbling with excitement.

CHAPTER 9

The New Girl
Danielle's Story

♥ ♥ ♥ ♥ ♥

A girl stepped through the front doorway. She wore a pretty blue-flowered dress. Her long, curly blond hair was tied back with a blue bow.

Her dress looks cheerful, said our maid. *But she does not.*

She appears to be about your age, Danielle, said Papa.

Eight, I said. I had always been eight.

In one hand, the girl held a small traveling case.

She hasn't got many clothes, judging by the size of her case, said Maman.

I saw Sophie's red curls bounce with laughter upstairs as she pointed at Evette's small traveling case. She whispered to the other girls. Their hair ribbons shook merrily as they all giggled.

Evette looked up at them in surprise. Then she lowered her eyes shyly.

"I have been expecting you," the schoolmistress told the visitors. "I have made tea. Please, do come in." She turned to lead the guests into the front room where we were.

They are coming this way! I shouted.

Now we will get to hear everything, the maid added gleefully.

Unfortunately, Madame Pumpkin did not budge. "I haven't much time before my train leaves. So I cannot stay for tea," she said in a bored voice.

"Oh," said the schoolmistress. She seemed a bit embarrassed that the lady had turned down her invitation. "Perhaps another time."

"Unlikely," said Madame Pumpkin. "I doubt I shall visit the school again."

"I see," the schoolmistress said uncertainly.

Then who will come visit Evette? I asked.

I am sure her parents will, said Maman.

All the girls lived at the school, except for the summer holidays. Still, their families came to visit now and then during the year.

While the two women spoke, Evette studied her surroundings. Her sad blue eyes showed a sparkle of interest when she spotted our dollhouse.

I studied Evette, too. I was filled with questions.

Who is she? I wondered. *Why is she so quiet? Do you think she likes dolls?*

Hush, Danielle, said Maman. *It is unladylike to be too curious.*

Who cares about being a lady? I asked.

Danielle, listen to your maman, said Papa. *She knows best.*

Yes, Papa, I said. But I didn't know why grown-ups always thought they knew best.

"As I told you in my letter, Evette's parents were killed in a train accident a month ago," Madame Pumpkin went on.

I gasped. *Poor Evette!*

How terrible! Maman said in a shocked voice.

Poor child, said Papa.

The girls on the stairs started whispering again. The word "orphan" drifted down to my ears.

The schoolmistress gazed at Evette with kind eyes. "Yes, I know. So awful —"

"Such a bother," said Madame Pumpkin. "My husband and I are distant relations of her father's. Since there was no one else to take her, Evette was sent to us. I have little interest in children, so it seemed best to bring her here."

"A wise decision. And she is welcome," began the schoolmistress.

"Yes. Yes. As long as there is money to pay the school's fee, she is welcome, no?" Madame Pumpkin said rudely. "Well, her mother was from England. So we shall see if she has any English relatives who will pay for her care after her small inheritance runs out. My husband and I will not use our own money to support her."

The schoolmistress looked flustered. "She will get a good education here, of course. I will teach her the skills it takes to be a lady. Her lessons will include embroidery, painting, music, manners, dancing —"

"Very well!" Madame Pumpkin waved a careless hand and turned to the door. "I must be going now."

Evette's frightened eyes darted to her relative. "Wait! Am I to stay here alone? But I don't know anyone . . ."

Madame Pumpkin tapped her silver-tipped umbrella and shook a warning finger at Evette. "Silence, girl! I want no trouble out of you. You will behave and learn your lessons."

Evette jumped at the harsh words. Her gaze sank to the floor. "Yes, Madame," she mumbled.

With a sharp twist of the doorknob, Madame Pumpkin was gone.

Briskly, the schoolmistress took Evette's hand and led her up the stairs. "Don't worry. You'll be fine here, my dear. Your lessons will keep you busy. And the other girls will make you feel welcome."

She looked up to the second-floor stairs. "Won't you, girls?"

Sophie smiled a fake smile at Evette from above. "Of course, Mistress."

CHAPTER 10
Moving Around
Danielle's Story

♥　♥　♥　♥　♥

The very next morning, Evette came to visit our doll-house.

She walked into the parlor slowly so the book lying flat on top of her head wouldn't fall off.

Very ladylike, Maman said in approval.

The fact that there was a book on her head did not surprise me. It is the way the schoolgirls were taught to walk gracefully. The schoolmistress did not allow them to run.

When Evette tilted her head, the book slid off into her hands.

I read its title. *"Alice's Adventures in Wonderland!" I have that very book on the dollhouse playroom bookshelf!*

Evette set the book on a chair and came close.

"Oh, my!" she said softly. "Where did such a wonderful dollhouse come from?"

Maman and Papa's smiles brightened at her words. They were proud of our home.

When Evette spied us in the dining room, she gave a happy squeak. "And little dolls, too!"

She looked at Maman and Papa. "Such a handsome lady and gentleman. Every home should have such fine parents."

What a lovely child, said Maman.

Quite so, agreed Papa.

Evette's gaze moved to our maid and butler. "And I am sure you both take good care of the household."

It's clever of her to appreciate our importance, said the maid.

Oui, said the butler.

"And what a pretty little brown-haired girl," Evette said, smiling at me. She curtseyed. "Bonjour!"

Bonjour, Mademoiselle Evette, I said politely.

Maman looked pleased by my good manners.

Evette studied the rooms in our house, one by one. She began with the kitchen on the floor below us.

The maid stiffened with worry. More than one of our Wedgwood plates had been broken by careless schoolgirls.

However, Evette only picked up a tiny copper cooking pot and a stirring spoon curiously. Then she put them back.

After that, she peeked at the food stored in our cellar. The biscuit tins, jam jars, and bags of flour were stacked in neat rows. She left them as she found them.

It's plain to see that she's a careful girl, said the maid.

Very tidy, the butler added.

Evette went room by room, examining our things. When she had seen the entire house, she returned to us in the dollhouse dining room.

She picked up Maman in one of her hands and Papa in her other. She held them side by side.

"Perhaps you would be more comfortable in the dollhouse parlor by the fire?" she asked them.

Oui! said Papa.

Yes, please, said Maman.

Evette moved them to the dollhouse parlor. She set Maman in the cushioned chair beside her embroidery hoop. Papa went in his favorite leather armchair. She even put his book in his hand.

At last! I can't wait to find out what new mischief Tom Sawyer is up to, said Papa. He began reading immediately.

Maman sat at her embroidery with a delighted smile on her face.

Next, Evette picked up our maid. She lifted her toward the attic. "Where is your bedroom?" she asked. "In the attic?"

She tilted the roof up on its hinges so she could put the maid in her attic room.

Oui! But I must go to the kitchen! said the maid. *I have work to do.*

Evette paused, lowering the roof again. "Or perhaps you would rather work in the kitchen?" She moved the maid downstairs into the dollhouse kitchen and stood her at the worktable. It was covered with mixing bowls and cooking ingredients.

Merci! said the maid.

The butler was next to be moved.

"I shall place you by the front doors of the dollhouse," Evette told him. She put him just inside the doors, at the top of the porch stairs. "There. Now you can greet important guests the moment they arrive."

A very proper arrangement, the butler replied. His stiff voice sounded approving.

Then Evette reached into the playroom on the fourth floor of the dollhouse. She pulled out my favorite doll, which was smaller than her thumb.

She picked me up from the dining room table. "I wonder if you would be happier in the playroom playing with this tiny doll?"

Oui! I would! I said.

She set me on a chair in the playroom, with my little doll in my lap.

We were all quite happy in our new places.

CHAPTER 11
Baggage
Danielle's Story

♥ ♥ ♥ ♥ ♥

T hat afternoon, the schoolmistress brought Evette into the parlor for music instruction.

The dollhouse maid sighed. *Another afternoon with girls banging the piano.*

We shall all have headaches before it's over, no doubt, said our butler.

At least we shall have company for a while, I said. *I never have any playmates.*

What about baby Henri and your pets? asked Maman.

Henri is too little to be much fun, I said. *And playing with Mimi and Fifi is not the same as playing with other girls.*

The schoolmistress sat on the piano bench and motioned for Evette to sit beside her. "This is our practice piano. The grand piano is next door in the music room. It is only for special occasions. Do you play?"

"A little," Evette answered, sitting down.

Very good, said Maman. *That is a proper answer. Ladies should never brag, whether they play well or not.*

"Please begin," said the schoolmistress.

Evette set her fingers on the keyboard. They moved swiftly along the keys.

Papa stopped reading. *Ah! Beethoven.*

It is a delightful tune, said Maman.

And she plays it well, said the butler.

The other schoolgirls gathered in the doorway to listen. Several of them danced and twirled to the unexpectedly fine concert.

Soon even the dollhouse maid was humming along with the music.

"My, you are quite skilled," said the schoolmistress when Evette finished. "Who was your instructor?"

"My papa. He was a concert pianist with the French opera," said Evette. "And my maman was a music teacher in England before she married him."

"Well, it was a pleasure to hear you," the schoolmistress told Evette. "Now I shall leave you to practice."

She waved the rest of the schoolgirls toward the stairs. "Let's get back to our English lessons!"

Three girls, Sophie, Nicole, and Claire, stayed behind. As soon as the schoolmistress was out of sight, Sophie sat on the piano bench and nudged Evette aside. "My turn," she said.

Evette didn't argue. She stood and wandered over to the dollhouse to pick me up.

The other two girls followed her, ignoring Sophie's performance.

"I wish I could play piano as well as you," Claire told Evette.

There is no sense in wishing for what we cannot have, Maman advised.

"You play even better than Sophie," Nicole added.

Sophie banged a loud, sour note on the piano. Her hard eyes glittered jealously.

Uh-oh, said the maid.

Until now, Sophie played the piano better than anyone at the school, said Maman.

This could be dangerous for Evette. Sophie likes to be the best, said Papa.

Claire sighed as she watched Evette comb my hair. "We've been so busy with lessons that we haven't played with the dollhouse in a while."

"Yes. It takes a lot of time to prepare for Visiting Day. In a few months, our parents will come to see what we have learned. We don't want to disappoint them," said Nicole.

Here comes trouble, muttered our butler.

Sophie joined the three girls. "Do you like the dollhouse?" she asked Evette.

Evette smiled at her. "Oh, yes! And this is my favorite doll. She is so sweet."

Merci, I said, blushing.

Sophie snatched me away from Evette. She looked down at me and frowned. "I think it's creepy the way these little dolls are always staring. I don't like them." She shivered and shoved me in the dollhouse cellar.

Wait! You have put me in the wrong room. I never go in here, I said. *It's too dark and lonely.*

Evette reached out to rescue me.

Sophie stood in front of our dollhouse, blocking her.

"I think they are a lovely family of dolls," said Evette. "And they have a beautiful home."

"Unlike you," said Sophie.

Evette stiffened.

"We heard what the lady who brought you here told the schoolmistress," said Sophie. "Right, girls?"

Claire and Nicole moved closer to Sophie.

"Right," said Nicole.

"Is it true that you're an orphan?" Claire asked.

Evette nodded.

"What's it like, not having a mother or a father?" asked Sophie.

Evette remained silent.

"Do you feel like unwanted baggage?" asked Sophie.

She picked up a small trunk from the dollhouse storage room and flicked it carelessly into the kitchen. It landed behind the maid, barely missing her.

No! No! scolded the maid. *Do not clutter up my kitchen with this trunk! Put it back where you got it.*

Sophie could not hear her. "I have worked hard on my music lessons to be ready for Visiting Day."

"Yes. Sophie has practiced the piano for many hours," agreed Nicole.

"It wouldn't be fair if you play better than she in front of our families," added Claire.

Sophie frowned at her.

"Not that you could!" Claire corrected herself quickly.

"Perhaps you should plan to stay in your room instead of performing," Sophie suggested to Evette. "Your family won't be coming. So no one will miss you."

"If you don't want me to play the piano on Visiting Day, I won't," said Evette.

Sophie looked surprised that she had agreed so easily. "Fine," she said. "I am glad you are willing to be reasonable. Come along, girls."

She left the room, and the other girls hurried after her.

Evette lifted me from among the bags of flour and set me in the dollhouse parlor with Maman and Papa.

Then she took the trunk Sophie had thumped into the kitchen and put it back where it belonged. She ran her fingers over the trunk's carved leather sides.

"Sophie is right," she whispered softly. "I am unwanted baggage."

CHAPTER 12

Forgetting

♥ ♥ ♥ ♥ ♥

Far Nana gasped, taking Rose and Lila by surprise. "I almost forgot! I promised to call the museum after the dollhouse arrived. I have some repair questions for them."

Rose checked the clock. "Tonight? It's almost ten o'clock."

"The museum doesn't close until ten-thirty, so I still have time," said Far Nana.

"Oh, c'mon," said Lila. "We can't stop when Evette's feeling so sad."

"I know. I'm sorry, girls. We'll have to continue the doll's story tomorrow," said Far Nana. She hurried down the hall toward the phone.

Rose and Lila headed for their room.

Once there, Rose couldn't sleep. She tossed and turned in her lower bunk bed until her quilt was tangled around her legs.

She had a funny feeling she had forgotten something. But what? She thought back over what had happened that evening.

After Far Nana had sent Lila and her off to bed, Rose remembered brushing her teeth. She and Lila had put on their pajamas. And then —

Suddenly, she remembered what she'd forgotten.

"Lila! Wake up," she whispered. She knocked on the underside of the upper bunk.

"What?" grumbled a sleepy voice above her.

"Did you kiss Mom and Dad good night?" Rose asked.

"Uh. No," said Lila. "I forgot." Now she sounded more awake.

"Me, too. Let's do it now," suggested Rose.

Quickly, they both snapped open the lockets their parents had given them before leaving for Africa. They kissed the photos of their mom and dad inside.

Snap! Snap! They shut their parents snugly away again.

"I can't believe we forgot," said Lila. "Do you think Mom and Dad ever forget us?"

Rose wondered the same thing, but she didn't want Lila to worry. "No. They probably miss us, though."

"I miss them, too," said Lila. "I wish they were coming to Parents' Night."

"Yeah," said Rose. "Without them it'll be No-Parents' Night."

"If we call them and beg, could they get here by Friday?" asked Lila.

"They won't come all the way from Africa just for Parents' Night," Rose told her.

"Well, at least Far Nana will be there with us," said Lila.

"Unless we accidentally on purpose forget to tell her about it," said Rose.

"Why would we do that?" asked Lila. "If she doesn't go, we can't go."

"So? That's better than being the only ones who show up without parents," said Rose.

"Isn't bringing a grandmother good enough?" asked Lila.

"It's called Parents' Night. Not Grandparents' Night," said Rose.

"Don't you want to show the school to Far Nana?" asked Lila.

Rose shrugged in the darkness. "Far Nana has to finish the dollhouse before next Monday. That's a lot of work to do in one week. She's going to be too busy to care about seeing our school."

Lila thought for a minute. "What about our Parents' Night projects? I'm making a beaver lodge with Kelly."

"We'll still have to do them to get good grades," said Rose. "But I think we should forget about going to Parents' Night."

CHAPTER 13

Supplies

♥   ♥   ♥   ♥   ♥

After school the next day, Far Nana, Rose, and Lila went shopping.

Far Nana had a list of things she needed to repair the dollhouse.

She bought wallpaper scraps at a home decorating store, beads and ribbon at a fabric store, and thin sheets of balsa wood at a model airplane shop.

Rose had a list of her own, so they also stopped at the grocery store. She got sugar cubes, eggs, and confectioners' sugar.

"It's for a school project," she told Far Nana.

Lila got cat treats from the pet food aisle.

"For the cats," she said. "Since they have to stay out of the doll hospital for a while."

When they got home, they had dinner. After they ate, they were all tired.

"Are we too tired to hear more of the doll's story?" Far Nana asked.

"No way," said Lila.

"Right," said Rose. "I want to know what happens to Evette and Danielle."

They went upstairs to the witch's hat, and Danielle's story continued.

CHAPTER 14
Cakes
Danielle's Story

♥ ♥ ♥ ♥ ♥

As the months passed, Evette spent her time at school, learning to be a lady. She practiced dancing and stitched embroidery samplers like the other girls. She studied French and English. And she painted watercolor portraits.

She visited us as often as she could between her lessons. One morning, the schoolmistress found her kneeling by the dollhouse. She was about to set me on the widow's walk on our dollhouse roof.

"Will you run an errand for me?" the schoolmistress asked.

"Oui," said Evette. She slipped me into her pocket and stood up.

"Go to the bakery by the park and purchase a dozen croissants for teatime," said the schoolmistress. "Charge it to the school's account."

"Oui, Mistress." Evette grabbed her bonnet and shawl and hurried outside.

Halfway down the block, she reached into her pocket and pulled me out.

"Did you think I put you in my pocket by mistake?" she asked, smiling. "No. I did it on purpose. I thought perhaps you would like to go on an adventure."

Oui, I would like that! I said.

"We shall take the long way to the bakery," said Evette. "It goes through the park. I have been this way many times on outings with the other schoolgirls."

She put me back in her pocket. I bounced happily inside as Evette skipped along the fern-covered park path.

"The schoolmistress would not approve if she saw me skipping," she said.

Neither would Maman, I said. *But it is fun!*

All too soon, we left the park and crossed a cobblestone lane lined with shops. Carts, carriages, and strolling ladies and gentlemen filled the busy boulevard.

Evette pulled me from her pocket so I could see the shops we passed. "This is the cobbler, this is the bank, and this is the hatmaker," she told me.

We paused to stare in a toy-shop window where rows of small metal soldiers stood with painted wooden horses. Fancy lady dolls sat on a lace-covered table. I saw a group of little china dollhouse dolls on a nearby shelf. One of them looked a lot like Papa. Before I could ask him if he might be a relative of mine, we were off again.

"And here is the bakery," Evette said at last. She stepped inside a charming shop and took a deep breath. I did, too.

Ooh-la-la! What a delicious smell! I said.

"I love the smell of baking bread," agreed Evette.

"Bonjour, Mademoiselle," the baker said in greeting. "What would you and your little doll like to buy?"

"Twelve croissants, please," said Evette. "Put them on the boarding school's account."

"Certainly. Wait one moment while I warm them up for you," he said.

"Merci," said Evette.

We wandered around the bakery to pass the time.

Bonjour, said two tiny voices from somewhere behind me.

I looked around to see who had spoken.

All I saw were cakes. There were at least two dozen of them on shelves nearby. Some were square and some were round. They were covered in swirls of chocolate, vanilla, or strawberry frosting.

One white cake towered above the rest. It was three layers tall and was decorated with silver bells and bows.

"What a lovely wedding cake!" said Evette. We went closer.

On the very top of it, two little china dolls — a man and a woman — stood holding hands. I realized it must have been they who had spoken.

Bonjour, I told them. *Why are you standing on a cake?*

We are a bride and groom, replied the woman.

We have stood upon at least fifty wedding cakes before this one, said the man.

How wonderful, I said. *Do you enjoy it?*

Oui! they replied happily. *Weddings are exciting, and there is always a party afterward.*

I have only been to birthday parties, said another tiny voice. *They are enjoyable, too.*

It was a little princess doll with a gown made of pink frosting. She stood on top of a pretty birthday cake, with flowers and leaves twined around its edges.

Evette leaned down to look at the princess birthday cake.

"My birthday is next Friday," she said.

I didn't know that, I said.

You should have a party, said the bride and groom dolls.

Yes! And I want to come. Please, buy my cake, suggested the princess doll.

I'm sorry, I told her. *We have no money to buy you.*

Oh, the princess said in disappointment.

"I just realized that my birthday is the day after the school's Visiting Day," said Evette. She spoke so softly

that only I heard. "It will be my first birthday since . . . since my parents —"

"Here you go!" called the baker.

Evette and I jumped at the sound of his hearty voice as he came up behind us.

He handed the box of croissants to Evette.

"Thank you, sir. Oh! It is getting late," she said, looking up at the clock on the wall. "We must hurry."

We rushed back to the school.

CHAPTER 15

Teatime

Danielle's Story

♥   ♥   ♥   ♥   ♥

In here!" the schoolmistress called when we returned. Evette followed the sound of her voice, and we found her in the parlor. The mistress, Sophie, and several other schoolgirls were in chairs around a small tea table near the dollhouse. A fancy china teapot with matching cups and saucers sat in the middle of the table.

The girls were preparing to practice the ladylike art of pouring tea.

Quickly, Evette slid me into her pocket.

Danielle? Are you there? asked Maman.

Yes, I called from inside the pocket. *We have been on an adventure. But I am safe.*

"Join us, Evette," the schoolmistress instructed.

Evette set the croissants on the table and sat in an empty chair. I was able to peek over the top edge of her pocket and watch.

"Sophie, you may pour," said the schoolmistress.

"Let Evette take a turn instead," suggested Sophie.

Awful girl. She is hoping Evette will be clumsy, I heard the dollhouse maid mutter.

I tensed, hoping Evette would perform well.

Evette picked up the teapot. She poured steaming tea into the dainty china teacups. She passed the cups and saucers to the others. Then she stirred her tea with a silver spoon. All without spilling a drop.

Well done! I heard Maman say.

"Excellent job," said the schoolmistress.

Sophie's hard eyes glared at Evette.

"We must also practice our polite conversation," the schoolmistress said. "Who would like to begin?"

"I will," said Sophie. She took a sip of tea. "As everyone knows, the summer holidays begin after Visiting Day. Will any of you be doing anything special?"

"My parents are coming to take me to the Louvre," said Nicole.

"A museum? How pleasant," said Sophie. She didn't sound like she meant it.

"My papa is going to take me for a boat ride on the Seine River," said Claire.

"Well!" Sophie interrupted importantly. "My maman is going to take me to the best dressmaker in Paris. I shall get a new gown!"

"You are so lucky! You are always getting new gowns," said Nicole.

Sophie smiled smugly.

They went on talking about their plans. Evette was silent.

"And you, Evette?" Sophie asked finally. "Where are you going for the holidays?"

Evette's teacup rattled in its saucer as she almost dropped it. "I am staying at the school."

"What about your parents?" asked Sophie. "Oh, I forgot. You don't have any parents, do you?"

"Sophie!" scolded the schoolmistress.

Evette just stared silently into her teacup.

CHAPTER 16
The Letter
Danielle's Story

♥ ♥ ♥ ♥ ♥

Someone is coming, our butler announced that afternoon.

The schoolgirls had long since finished their tea and gone upstairs for lessons. I was back in the dollhouse, playing with my poodle, Fifi. We were all together in the dollhouse parlor. Even baby Henri was in Maman's arms. It was quite cozy.

As the butler's words died away, a letter slipped through the metal slot in the school's front door. It slid across the marble floor to rest at the bottom of the staircase.

Who sent it? asked our maid. *To whom is it addressed? Can anyone see?*

It's sealed with purple wax, said the butler. *I cannot read the address from here.*

Now, now. I am sure it is not for us, said Maman. *And we should not read other people's mail.*

A moment later, Sophie came downstairs. She saw

the letter, picked it up, and read the address. She carried it into the parlor and shut the door behind her.

Then she lit a candle on a nearby desk and held the letter so the flame heated the wax seal. When it softened enough, she opened the letter and began reading.

Now I could see the address on the front.

It is addressed to the schoolmistress, I said. *Not to Sophie. She is snooping!*

Such bad manners! said Maman.

At least she'll find out what's in the letter, said the maid. *That's more than we can say.*

After Sophie finished reading, she folded the letter and smiled sneakily.

That smile means trouble, I'll wager, said Papa.

The parlor door opened and Evette came in. She headed toward our dollhouse, not noticing Sophie.

"Hello, my friends," she told us.

"Dolls are your only friends around here," said Sophie. She hid the letter behind her back.

Evette whirled around. "Sophie! I'm sorry — I didn't see you. I shall come back later." She turned to leave.

"A letter came from your relative today," Sophie said quickly.

Evette stopped in surprise. "How do you know?"

"I have my ways," said Sophie.

Meddling ways, said Maman.

"Where is it?" asked Evette.

Sophie just smirked.

"Please tell me!" Evette begged.

I heard the schoolmistress's heels click across the marble floor outside the parlor.

Sophie heard, too. She shoved Evette. At the same time, I saw her secretly slide the letter into the pocket of Evette's dress.

"What are you doing?" Evette asked, startled. She pushed Sophie back, then fell against our dollhouse, knocking it off the cabinet.

Look out! I shouted.

The dollhouse fell to the floor. Our furniture slid every which way. I bounced out of the dollhouse onto the carpet. My family did, too.

Is everyone all right? Papa asked when the excitement was over.

My arm is a bit chipped, I told him. *But my pets are okay.*

The lace on my hem is torn, and my hair is mussed. Nothing very terrible, said Maman. *And baby Henri is unharmed.*

I am fine, said the butler.

I am, too, said the maid. *But the dollhouse is a mess!*

The schoolmistress rushed in and saw our house on the carpet.

"Girls!" she scolded. "What happened to the doll-house? Come, help me pick it up."

The three of them lifted our house and set it back on the cabinet. We still lay in a jumble on the carpet, with our furniture.

"Now, what is all this shouting about?" the schoolmistress asked. "Ladies do not raise their voices."

"Yes, of course, Mistress," Sophie said. She smiled her fake smile. "Evette has much to learn. For instance, that she should not read other people's mail."

"What?" asked the schoolmistress.

Evette held out her empty hands, palms up. "I didn't read anyone else's mail."

"I saw her put a letter addressed to you in her pocket, Mistress," Sophie fibbed.

CHAPTER 17

News
Danielle's Story

♥ ♥ ♥ ♥ ♥

Evette pulled the letter from her pocket and stared at it in surprise. She handed it to the schoolmistress.

"I don't know how it got there," she said.

The schoolmistress took the letter and hastily read it. When she finished, she looked worried.

"Sophie, you may leave now," she said. "Evette and I have business to discuss."

Sophie smiled. "Of course, Mistress." She curtseyed and left the room, humming happily.

"I didn't read the letter. Truly," said Evette.

"It doesn't matter, dear," the schoolmistress replied softly. "This letter is from your relative, so it concerns you anyway. It is not good news, I'm afraid. You will have to be brave."

Evette hugged herself, looking frightened.

"Your inheritance has run out, so there is no more money to pay for your schooling," the schoolmistress went on. "Your relative has arranged for you to be sent to a workhouse."

"A workhouse?" Evette echoed in disbelief. She sat down quickly. "I thought those were only in England."

"The letter says that because your mother was English, a workhouse there has agreed to accept you," said the schoolmistress.

"Is it true what they say about workhouses?" Evette asked in a shaky voice. "Are they really dirty, dangerous places? Will I have to work long hours in a factory or b-b-become a ragpicker?"

She began to sob.

I lay silent on the carpet, shocked by the news.

The schoolmistress sat by Evette and put a comforting hand on her arm. "I have grown fond of you. If there were any way to keep you here, I would. But I don't own the school, so I cannot let you stay without payment. I'm afraid you must do as your relative wishes."

"How long will I have to stay there?" asked Evette.

"You may leave when you turn twenty-one," said the schoolmistress. "Until then, the workhouse will give you clothes, food, and shelter in exchange for the work you do."

Maman! Papa! Something must be done to prevent Evette from being sent away, I shouted at last.

Calm down, Danielle. We are only tiny dolls, said Maman. *What can we do?*

She mustn't go to a horrid workhouse. She can't! I insisted.

After a time, the schoolmistress left to attend to her duties. Evette sat alone for a few moments. Then she stood and walked slowly toward the door.

I don't want you to go, I whispered.

Suddenly, Evette turned and hurried back to our dollhouse. "I am sorry! I almost forgot about you. Is everyone all right?" she asked us.

She knelt down, picked us up, and set us on the cabinet beside our empty house.

We are fine. I only hope the house isn't damaged, said Papa.

"It looks like you are all unharmed. But one corner of the dollhouse roof is slightly crumpled. And the stair railing is broken," said Evette. "I'm sorry."

She began to put our furniture back in place, piece by piece.

"Did you hear the news?" she whispered. "I must leave the school and go to a workhouse!"

Yes, it is terrible news, Papa agreed.

Simply awful, said Maman.

"I will miss you all so much!" Evette gazed at me sadly as she put me in my bedroom. "You most of all, my little friend."

I will miss you, too, I told her.

CHAPTER 18
Concentrating

♥ ♥ ♥ ♥ ♥

Far Nana stood and arched her back to stretch. She set the metal tool she was holding on her worktable.

Rose and Lila groaned. They knew what was coming.

"I've got to concentrate on my repair work for a while," Far Nana said. "So you girls had better —"

"Do your homework," said Rose.

"Then go to bed," added Lila.

Far Nana smiled. "Right."

Rose and Lila opened the witch's hat door and shut it behind them. They headed down the hall.

Hours later, Rose got up from bed to get a drink of water. She saw a light under the witch's hat door. Far Nana was still working on the dollhouse in the middle of the night!

CHAPTER 19
Class Projects

♥ ♥ ♥ ♥ ♥

The next day after school, Bart and Lila's friend from second grade, Kelly, walked home with Rose and Lila.

"Are you Rose's boyfriend?" Kelly asked Bart.

"No!" Rose and Bart answered at the same time.

"He's just coming over to work on our Parents' Night project," said Rose.

"That's why I'm coming over, too," said Kelly. "Second grade is doing animal habitats."

"We're making our beaver lodge out of mud and sticks," said Lila. "In the backyard."

"It's almost done," added Kelly.

"Everybody's project is almost done, except ours," said Rose. She gave Bart The Eye.

"Ours will get done in time," said Bart. "We have two nights to finish."

"Why did you wait so long to start working on it?" asked Kelly.

"We like living dangerously," said Bart.

"Speak for yourself," asked Rose. "I don't like being in danger of getting a big fat F on this project."

"We won't," said Bart as they turned onto the sidewalk to Far Nana's house.

Rose, Lila, and Kelly went up the steps to the front porch. Bart followed slowly, staring at the house.

"Is this where you live?" he asked.

"Yeah," said Rose.

"It's our grandmother's house," said Lila. "Cool, huh?"

Bart looked up. "What's in that weird room with the pointy roof?"

"That's the witch's hat," said Lila. "It's full of dolls."

"Dolls?" echoed Bart. "Ick."

"I bet I know a doll you'd like," said Rose.

"No way," said Bart.

"How about a Danger Ranger action figure? I saw some in a store," said Rose.

"Really? Cool," said Bart. "But those aren't dolls."

"Are too," said Lila.

"See? I guess you do like dolls," said Rose.

"So do I," said Kelly. "Can we go up and see the ones in the witch's hat?"

"Sure," said Lila. "My grandmother is fixing a dollhouse for a museum right now."

"Cool!" said Kelly.

They all went inside and put their backpacks on the hall table.

Lila took Kelly upstairs.

Rose wished she could go with them. Instead, she led Bart into the kitchen.

She got out the supplies she'd bought at the grocery store the day before.

"What's all that?" Bart asked when he saw the things Rose put on the kitchen table.

"Stuff to make an igloo," she said. "Sugar cubes, eggs, and confectioners' sugar. A cardboard circle for the base, and paintbrushes."

"I wanted to make a teepee," Bart complained.

Rose put her hands on her hips and glared at him. "Did you bring the stuff to make one?"

"No," said Bart.

"Then I guess we're making an igloo," said Rose.

Bart sighed and sat down. "Guess so."

Rose cracked the eggs and let the clear part of them fall into a bowl. "First, we mix the egg whites and the sugar. That makes glue. We paint the glue on the cubes, and that'll make them stick together."

"How did you figure out how to do this?" Bart asked, sounding more interested.

"I got the instructions on the Internet when I used the library computer," said Rose.

She painted the egg-and-sugar glue around the edge of the cardboard circle.

Together, she and Bart made a ring of sugar cubes. Then they painted glue on the top of that row.

"Set the next row of cubes closer to the center. We'll move them in a little closer each time we make a row," she told Bart. "That way it will make a rounded roof."

"Do you like living with your grandmother?" Bart asked as he stacked cubes.

Rose shrugged. "Yeah."

"How long are you going to live with her?" he asked.

"For the rest of the year," said Rose.

"Are your parents ever coming back?" he asked.

"Yes," she said.

"When?" asked Bart.

"Like I said — at the end of the year," said Rose.

Bart opened his mouth to ask another question. But Rose was faster.

"Hungry?" she asked. "How about some carob corn? It's like candy corn, only chocolate-flavored and more healthy."

Without waiting for Bart to answer, she went to the cupboard and got some carob corn. She gave it to Bart to keep his mouth busy. Maybe that would stop him from asking so many questions.

Rose heard Lila and Kelly talking outside as they

Milk
tomatoes
corn

Confectioner
Suger

worked on their beaver lodge. After a while, Lila came into the kitchen to wash her muddy hands.

Then she leaned her elbows on the table to stare at their project. "Do Eskimos still live in igloos?"

Rose shook her head no. "My history book at school says they live in regular houses and apartments now."

"They still build igloos to stay in when they're hunting, though," added Bart.

"*Brrr!* Who would want to live in a house made of ice?" asked Lila.

"I would," said Bart. "It sounds dangerous."

"Not me," said Lila. "It would be like living in a refrigerator. I'd rather live in a house made of sugar cubes. Yum!"

Rose laughed and handed Lila some carob corn. "How's your beaver lodge going?"

"Done," said Lila. "Kelly went home."

"Look! I've got beaver teeth," Bart joked. He smiled, showing two carob corn triangles stuck onto his front teeth.

Lila giggled.

All of a sudden, Ringo jumped onto the table, twitching his tail. He tried to grab a sugar cube in his teeth and zoom away. The table jiggled. The half-finished sugar cube igloo Rose and Bart had built caved in without a sound.

Rose stared at the mess. "Oh, no!" she wailed. "Now we'll never finish in time."

"In time for what?" asked Far Nana, coming into the kitchen. She saw the pile of sugar cubes on the table. "What's that?"

"Don't ask," said Rose.

"Their igloo caved in," said Lila.

"We're going to have to start over," said Rose. She glared at Bart. "See what I told you about waiting till the last minute?"

"I'll come over again tomorrow," said Bart. "We still have another night to finish. Parents' Night isn't until Friday." He grabbed his backpack and headed out the door.

Lila elbowed Rose. "You forgot to introduce Bart to Far Nana."

Rose rolled her eyes.

CHAPTER 20
No Big Deal

♥ ♥ ♥ ♥ ♥

"What's Parents' Night?" asked Far Nana as the door clicked shut behind Bart.

"It's no big deal," said Rose.

"It's okay if you can't come," said Lila.

"Is it one of those nights when your family visits your school to see what you've been learning?" asked Far Nana.

"Yeah," said Rose.

Lila nodded.

"Why didn't you tell me about it?" asked Far Nana.

"We thought you might be too busy to come," said Rose.

"And we didn't know if we could bring you," said Lila. "It's Parents' Night, and you're a grandparent."

Far Nana looked surprised.

"I'm sure you can bring me," she said. "I know your mom and dad would love to be there, too, if they could."

"But they can't!" said Rose. "They're never here when we need them."

Lila slipped her hand in Rose's. "We miss them."

"I miss them, too," said Far Nana.

Rose and Lila glanced at each other. They had never thought about how their grandmother might feel about their parents being gone.

"Tell you what," said Far Nana. "I'll take a camera. We'll mail photos of Parents' Night to your mom and dad. Then they can see what you've been up to at school."

"Does that mean you're coming on Friday?" asked Lila.

Far Nana took Rose's and Lila's free hands and squeezed them. "You betcha."

"Yay!" said Lila.

Rose smiled. But she wasn't sure whether to be glad. Or not.

CHAPTER 21
Messy

♥ ♥ ♥ ♥ ♥

After they finished the rest of their homework, Rose and Lila went upstairs to the witch's hat. The door was shut, so they knocked.

"Come in! Unless you're cats, that is," Far Nana called.

Rose and Lila went in.

"We're kids," Lila assured her.

"Close the door behind you so those furry varmints don't sneak in," said Far Nana.

The girls shut the door, and Rose stared in amazement.

The doll hospital was a wreck. Every available spot was filled with supplies and tools. There were jars of paint, varnish, and wax. There were paintbrushes, fabric, ribbons, tape, rulers, boxes of beads, and rolls of wallpaper and gift wrap.

"What a mess!" Rose whispered to Lila. "Do you think she'll be finished on time?"

"I don't know. Now the dollhouse looks worse than it did before," Lila whispered back.

Far Nana overheard. "Things always look worse before they look better in the doll hospital business. I've removed damaged areas of the roof and walls. I'm using sandpaper to smooth the floors. It'll all be lovely when it's freshly varnished or painted."

They watched as Far Nana dabbed glue on a toothpick. She used the toothpick to transfer a bit of glue onto a tiny bead. Then she stuck the bead on a dollhouse dresser drawer.

"You turned a bead into a drawer knob," said Lila. "Cool!"

"One of the tricks of the trade," said Far Nana.

She began rubbing Danielle's arm with a fingernail file.

Lila leaned closer to watch. "Why are you doing that?"

"Her arm is chipped. It's easier to sand small dolls and furniture with this little file than with a big piece of sandpaper. After her arm is sanded smooth, I'll give it a paint touch-up."

"Can we help?" asked Rose.

Far Nana shook her head no. "This is delicate work. I'd better do it."

"Oh," Rose said in disappointment.

"I know something else you could do to help, though," said Far Nana. She handed them a box full of small, curved pieces of wood.

Lila picked some up and let them dribble through her fingers and back into the box. "These look like toenails."

Far Nana laughed. "They're dollhouse roof shingles. I cut them out of balsa wood with a craft knife. They need to be painted to match the other shingles."

"We can paint them," said Lila.

"Yeah," said Rose.

Far Nana smiled. "Groovy."

Rose frowned. She hoped Far Nana didn't say any embarrassing hippie stuff like that on Parents' Night.

"Do you have time to do more of the doll story tonight?" asked Lila.

"Sure. We can work while we listen," said Far Nana.

She handed paintbrushes to them, and they started painting little roof shingles.

Far Nana painted, glued, and polished.

And Danielle continued her story.

CHAPTER 22
Music
Danielle's Story

♥ ♥ ♥ ♥ ♥

At long last, it was Visiting Day at the boarding school. Ten families had come to see what their daughters had learned. All morning, the schoolgirls had shown off their skills. They had sketched, poured tea, spoken English, and curtseyed.

Now they and their families were all in the music room, around the school's best piano. We listened as yet another schoolgirl banged on the piano keys.

Will this noise never end? grumbled our maid.

It is rather unmelodic at times, agreed the butler.

It is natural for parents to wish to see their daughters display their talents, said Maman.

But not all of these girls have a talent for piano! said the maid.

There was a moment of silence. Then another girl began to play.

Is it Evette this time? I asked.

Papa listened closely. *No. The musician is not quite as flawless as Evette. I believe it is Sophie.*

When will it be Evette's turn? I asked.

She promised Sophie she wouldn't play, said Maman.

That's right, said Papa. *And I don't think she is the kind of girl who would break a promise.*

Oh, I said, disappointed.

Just then, Evette entered the parlor and walked over to our dollhouse. "Hello, my friends."

Are you really not going to play? I asked.

"As you know, I promised Sophie I wouldn't play the piano on Visiting Day," said Evette.

No fair! I said.

"But —" Evette grinned and leaned closer. "I didn't promise not to sing, did I?" she whispered.

No, you didn't! I said.

She took a deep breath and started singing.

Her clear voice filled the room, making it somehow brighter and more cheerful. The sounds of Sophie's piano notes seemed to fade in the distance.

Your voice is extraordinary! said Papa. *It is a treat to hear it.*

I didn't even know you could sing! I told her.

She doesn't brag about her talents, like some girls we know, said Maman.

The melody is so pretty, it almost makes me want to weep, said the butler.

The maid sniffed. She *was* weeping!

The last note of Evette's beautiful song eventually died away.

If only everyone else could have heard you, I said.

Suddenly, we heard clapping like we'd never heard before. The parlor doors burst open, and dozens of people rushed in.

"How lovely!" said one of the parents.

"Your song was exquisite!" said another.

Everyone rushed to compliment Evette on her singing. Even Sophie's parents.

Evette turned pink as she listened to the praise and congratulations.

"Why didn't you sing in the music room with the others?" someone asked. It was Sophie's maman.

Sophie stiffened, afraid that Evette would tattle.

Evette smiled kindly at her. "I was just singing a song for myself," she said.

Evette looked at the dollhouse. I knew she had sung her song for us, too.

CHAPTER 23

The Birthday Wish

Danielle's Story

♥ ♥ ♥ ♥ ♥

The next morning, Evette appeared in the doorway of the parlor. She looked both ways in the hall behind her, then shut the doors and came to the dollhouse.

"Today is my birthday!" she announced. "I have come to celebrate it with you."

Happy birthday, I said. The other dolls bid her happy birthday as well.

Evette began to move us one by one into the dollhouse dining room. She set Maman, Papa, and me at the table. My pets, Mimi and Fifi, were placed by our feet. She stood the maid and butler nearby. She even brought baby Henri and his bed down for the occasion.

By the time she finished, silent tears were sliding down her cheeks.

Why are you crying? I asked.

"Today is also the day I must leave you," said Evette.

Leave? I echoed in dismay. *Oh, no!*

"My relative is coming for me this morning," she

said. "She is going to take me to the workhouse in England."

We shall miss you, dear child, said Maman.

It will be sad to say good-bye, said Papa.

A few tears squeezed from Evette's eyes and she wiped them away. "I refuse to be sad. Birthdays should be happy occasions."

She smiled a shaky smile.

"I have a surprise for you," she said to me. "I don't know when your birthday really is, but let's pretend today is your birthday, too. We shall both turn nine years old."

Ooh-la-la! I said happily. *I have been eight for so long. And I have always wanted to be nine.*

There is so much to do, said the maid. *We've never had a birthday party in the dollhouse before.*

"I have come prepared," said Evette. "I have made party decorations. There isn't much time. So let's get started."

She lay a little pink tablecloth on the dollhouse dining room table.

"This was my maman's lace handkerchief," she told us. "It still smells like her perfume. It helps me to hold it sometimes when I feel sad."

It is truly lovely, said my maman.

"I have also brought my papa's gold pocket watch,"

Evette went on. "It was his favorite. I think he would be pleased to see it hanging in your dollhouse."

She hung the watch behind Papa's chair in the parlor.

It is a fine timepiece, said Papa. *We are proud to have it in our home.*

"Now, let's set the table," suggested Evette.

We must use the best china dollhouse plates, said the maid.

And the best silver, said the butler.

Evette set little plates, forks, knives, spoons, and crystal glasses from our kitchen on the tablecloth in front of each of us. She set our largest round platter in the center of the table.

"And now I have the best surprise of all," she said.

Evette reached into the pocket of her blue-flowered dress and pulled something out. She placed it on the platter. "Voilà!"

It's a tiny cake! I said. *Where did you find it?*

"I made this little cake myself," she said. "It is only painted cardboard, but I tried to make it look like the pretty birthday cake we saw at the bakery. It is adorable, is it not!?"

Yes, it is the most beautiful cake I have ever seen! I said.

The painted cake had pink icing, with rosettes and green leaves made of paper. Nine tiny pink candles sat on the top. Each one was made from the end of a tooth-pick and was no longer than my hand.

Someone's coming, warned the butler.

The school's doorbell rang almost immediately.

Evette stiffened and looked toward the door.

A woman stood outside on the school's front porch. I could see her shadow through the lace curtains on the window.

"It must be my relative," Evette said in a frightened voice.

She turned back to the dollhouse.

"Hurry, my friend," she told me. "I must go to the workhouse. But first, we shall blow out our candles and make a wish."

Evette knelt beside our dollhouse, so her face was level with mine. The cake sat between us on the dining room table.

Look at the candles! our maid shouted suddenly.

We all gasped in amazement.

The tiny candles had not been lit. Not by any matchstick, at least. And yet their tips had begun to glow as though lit by tiny flames.

"Ready?" Evette asked me.

Yes, I said.

In the distance, I heard the schoolmistress open the school's front door.

Evette closed her eyes. "I wish I had a family," she whispered.

I wish you wouldn't go, I whispered at the same time.

Evette blew softly.

I blew toward the candles as well.

And then — something magical occurred. I cannot tell you exactly how it happened.

But when the schoolmistress and Evette's relative came into the parlor a moment later, they found it empty.

Evette was gone.

They searched and searched.

But they never found her.

CHAPTER 24

What Happened?

♥   ♥   ♥   ♥   ♥

After Danielle's story ended, there was silence in the witch's hat.

"Where did Evette go?" Rose asked finally.

"She didn't have to go to the workhouse, did she?" asked Lila.

"I've told you all I know," said Far Nana. "Now I've got more work to do on the dollhouse. So go get ready for bed."

Rose looked at Far Nana. Her skirt was wrinkled and her long, braided gray hair looked a little scraggly.

"Do you *have* to stay up late to work again?" Rose asked her.

"Yeah. You look kind of tired," said Lila.

"Gee, thanks," said Far Nana.

"Are you sure you're going to have time to go to Parents' Night with us?" asked Rose. "You don't have to, you know."

"I'll make time. Don't worry about the dollhouse,"

said Far Nana. "I'll get it finished before Monday. Now scoot."

A few minutes later, Rose and Lila were in their bedroom.

Lila slipped her pajama top over her head. "What do you think happened to Evette?"

Rose brushed her hair, until she had an idea. "Maybe she ran away. Maybe she found some money and went to live somewhere nice."

"Where would she find money?" asked Lila.

"I don't know. Maybe she sold her father's watch?" said Rose.

"Or maybe the woman at the door was really a rich relative from England who came to rescue her!" said Lila.

Rose sighed. "I hate not knowing what happened. I wish we could find out."

Lila grinned. "Maybe if we both wish at the same time, your wish will come true."

Rose grinned back. "Doubt it."

CHAPTER 25

No-Parents' Night

♥ ♥ ♥ ♥ ♥

The halls of Oak Hill Elementary were lit up when Rose, Lila, and Far Nana entered the school on Friday night.

Far Nana was wearing a flowing purple skirt and even more bead necklaces than usual. Her long braid was tied with a flowered green scarf.

Rose crossed her fingers. She hoped Far Nana wouldn't say or do anything embarrassing in front of the teachers and the other kids.

"The school looks creepy at night, oui?" Lila asked. She had been pretending to be French all day.

Rose looked in the office as they passed. The principal and the secretaries were gone, and the office was dark. "You're right. It is kind of creepy."

"What should we do first?" Far Nana asked.

Lila hopped in excitement. "Let's go to my classroom," she begged.

"Fine with me," said Rose.

When they got to Lila's class, it was already full of second-graders and their parents.

"Ooh-la-la!" said Lila. "C'mon, Far Nana. I have to introduce you to my teacher. You, too, Rose."

Rose read what was written on the chalkboard as they passed it.

PARENTS' NIGHT PROGRAM

1. Introduce your guests to the teacher.
2. Show them your Animal Habitat project.
3. Show them your creative writing folder and All About Me book.
4. Show them your desk and cubby.
5. Show them our class calendar, helpers chart, and book nook.

Lila tugged Far Nana and Rose toward her teacher. "Monsieur Yi!" she yelled. She waved at him across the room. Everyone turned to stare.

Rose groaned. She didn't have to wait for Far Nana to embarrass her. Lila had already done it.

When they stood in front of Mr. Yi, Lila curtseyed. "Bonsoir, Monsieur Yi. Thees eez is my grand-maman, and thees eez my sister, Mademoiselle Rose."

"Bonsoir, Mademoiselle Lila," said Mr. Yi. "What an unusual introduction."

"I wanted my introduction to be different," said Lila.

"It was," said Mr. Yi. "How do you say 'good job' in French?"

"Good job in French," Lila said, with a grin.

Suddenly, Far Nana whipped an instant camera out of her macramé purse. "Smile!" she said.

Mr. Yi and Lila smiled, and she snapped their picture.

Next, Lila dragged them off to see the Animal Habitat projects.

There were bear dens, crocodile nests, wombat burrows, and a beaver lodge. Above the projects was a sign that said ANIMALS NEED FOOD, WATER, SHELTER, AND SPACE.

"Beavers make homes from the branches of deciduous trees packed together with mud. They eat twigs, leaves, soft bark, and plants like cattails," Lila informed them.

Far Nana took a picture of Lila and her project.

After Lila showed them around for a while, it was time to visit Rose's fourth-grade classroom.

The minute they stepped into Rose's class, they ran into Emma and a gray-haired man wearing a peace sign button.

"Howdy," he said. "I'm George, Emma's grandfather."

"Bonsoir," said Lila. "I'm Mademoiselle Lila. Thees eez is my grand-maman, and thees eez my sister, Rose."

"Hi," mumbled Rose.

Far Nana smiled and made a peace sign with her fingers. "Groovy button, George."

Emma's grandfather grinned.

Emma looked at Far Nana's camera. "I wish *we'd* brought a camera."

"Don't worry. I have a photographic memory," her grandfather said. "There's only one problem with it."

"What?" asked Lila.

"Sometimes it runs out of film," said George.

He, Far Nana, and Lila laughed.

Emma scrunched up her face. "Gramps, you are so embarrassing sometimes."

George just laughed harder.

Nadia and another fourth-grader named Kiko came over in time to hear.

"My stepdad is even more embarrassing," Kiko whispered to Emma. "He wore his goofy plaid pants tonight."

"That's nothing," added Nadia. "My mom just told Ms. Bean that I slept with my cousin's dog in its doghouse one time when I was little! Can you believe it?"

Everybody's embarrassed about their families, thought Rose. Not just me. And not everyone brought a mom and a dad.

She and Lila went over to the project shelf. Bart was showing their igloo to his mother.

"Dangerous, huh?" he was asking.

"If that means 'good,' then yes," she said.

"It *does* look good," Lila whispered to Rose.

"Thanks." Rose had stayed up late the night before to finish it. She had sprinkled the last of the confectioners' sugar around the cardboard ground to make fake snow.

"Rose and I made it," Bart told his mom. "She has cool ideas."

Rose looked at Bart in surprise.

"Smile!" said Far Nana. She snapped several photos of Rose and Bart with their igloo.

While Far Nana talked to Rose's teacher for a while, Rose took Lila to the Which Star Am I? display.

"See if you can guess which star I am," Rose said.

Lila studied the silhouette heads on the stars. She guessed two wrong before she finally picked out Rose's.

Then Lila pointed to Bart's. "This one is definitely Bart."

Rose looked at the spiky hair on Bart's silhouette and grinned. "What gave it away?"

They both giggled.

CHAPTER 26
Package

♥ ♥ ♥ ♥ ♥

The next morning, Rose sorted through the instant photos Far Nana had taken at school. In one, Bart was making bunny ears behind Rose's head. Rose was giving him The Eye. She put that photo aside.

She picked up one of Far Nana, Lila, and her. Emma's grandfather had taken it. She glued it in the middle of a yellow poster. Then she picked the best of the other photos and glued them on around it.

At the bottom of the poster, she wrote,

> DEAR MOM AND DAD:
> WE LOVE YOU.
> DON'T FORGET US.

She drew hearts and flowers along the edges of the poster.

"What are you doing?" Lila asked Rose.

"Making a Parents' Night poster to send to Mom and Dad. I glued on some of the pictures Far Nana took last night. And see these flowers I drew all around the edges? They're *forget*-me-nots. That's the name of the flower. Get it?"

"Cool. Let me write something," said Lila. She picked up a marker.

Rose held the poster out of Lila's reach. "What are you going to write?"

"You'll see," said Lila.

Rose handed it to Lila. "Okay, but don't mess it up," she warned.

"I won't." Under Rose's message, Lila wrote,

DEAR MOM AND DAD:
U R 2 SWEET
2 B 4 GOTTEN

She thought a second. Then in big letters across the top of the poster, she wrote a title: FAMILY NIGHT.

Rose smiled. "Right. Because Parents' Night wasn't just for parents after all."

CHAPTER 27

Puzzle

♥ ♥ ♥ ♥ ♥

"Finished!" Far Nana announced Saturday afternoon. Rose and Lila looked at the dollhouse on Far Nana's worktable.

The corner of its roof wasn't crumpled anymore. The paint on its walls wasn't chipped. The stair railing was straight. The candlesticks were polished. The wooden floor shone with beeswax. And the wallpaper was fresh and clean.

Far Nana had stayed up late five nights in a row to finish it on time.

"The house looks great," said Rose.

"Bee-yoo-tee-ful. Especially the roof shingles we painted," said Lila.

"Yeah," agreed Rose.

They high-fived, giggling.

"It does look nice," said Far Nana. "But I still have the feeling something is missing."

"Like what?" Rose studied the dollhouse. "Maman

and Papa are in the parlor. Baby Henri is in the nursery. The maid is in the kitchen."

"The butler's by the door," Lila went on. "And Danielle, the dog, and the cat are all in the playroom."

Far Nana shrugged. "I don't know. It's just a funny feeling I have. As though the house is a puzzle with a piece missing."

Rose looked around the floor and shelves in the doll hospital. "I don't see any leftover furniture we forgot to put in or anything."

"I'm probably just tired," said Far Nana. "I'm going to go call the museum and tell them to expect the dollhouse on Monday. Then I've got four hours to get the house packed up before the delivery truck comes for it."

She left the room, shutting the door behind her.

"Nothing like finishing at the last minute," said Rose. "And after working on that igloo until right before Parents' Night — I mean Family Night — I should know."

Lila stared at the dollhouse and sighed. "I wish we could keep it."

"Me, too," said Rose. "But like Danielle's maman said, there's no sense in wishing for what we can't have."

"Hey, look," said Lila. She picked up a brochure from Far Nana's desk and opened it.

"It's a brochure about the museum where the dollhouse will go," said Rose.

"Wow! There are lots of dollhouses there already. Danielle and her family are going to fit right in," said Lila.

Rose looked at the photos in the brochure closely. "They aren't all houses. Some of them are stores. There's a hat shop, a market, a shoemaker, and a bookshop."

"Danielle's papa will like that," said Lila.

"And there's a doll school. Danielle will like that," said Rose. "She'll have other little girl dolls to hang out with."

"Cool!" said Lila.

CHAPTER 28
Number Nine

♥ ♥ ♥ ♥ ♥

Rose opened the door to the hall.

A black cat dashed past her, ran inside the doll hospital, and jumped on top of a high shelf.

"Ringo!" scolded Rose. "Shoo!"

"What's that?" asked Lila, pointing at his face.

Rose looked closer. A wad of white paper was dangling from the black cat's mouth. "It's tissue paper," she said. "With legs sticking out of it!"

"It's a dollhouse doll, wrapped in tissue!" yelled Lila.

"It can't be," said Rose. "All the dolls are in the house already."

"I don't care. I'm telling you, he's got another one," said Lila. "Don't let him get away!"

Rose shut the door to the witch's hat so the cat couldn't escape.

Lila found a curly piece of ribbon and wiggled it along the floor. "Here, Ringo!" she called.

Ringo dropped his tissue paper bundle on Far Nana's worktable and pounced on the ribbon.

Rose grabbed the bundle. "Eew! It's covered with cat slobber."

"Who cares? Let's see what's inside! Hurry." Lila picked Ringo up and gave him a quick pat. Then she put him out in the hall and closed the door again.

Rose unwrapped the tissue and pulled out — a doll!

"You were right! It *is* another dollhouse doll," she said. She held it up so Lila could see. It was wearing a flowered dress and tiny blue shoes.

"What a cute little girl," said Lila. "Where did it come from?"

Rose snapped her fingers. "I bet Ringo stole it from the red velvet box when we unpacked it that first day."

Lila patted the doll's blond hair. "Poor catnapped doll."

She set it in the playroom beside Danielle.

"Now there are nine dolls," said Rose.

"Danielle said only eight were made for the dollhouse," said Lila.

Rose nodded. "So who is this one?"

"Its dress has blue flowers like . . ." began Lila.

"It has blond hair like . . ." Rose said at the same time.

"Evette!?" they shouted.

"Do you think it's her?" Lila asked in a hushed voice.

"How could it be?" said Rose. "She was a real girl."

Lila elbowed her. "Remember Evette's birthday

wish? She wished for a family. And Danielle wished Evette wouldn't leave."

"Yeah. But Evette *couldn't* have turned into a doll," said Rose.

The girls stared at the dolls.

Danielle and the blond girl doll in the blue-flowered dress smiled secret smiles.

"Or could she?" Rose whispered.

Glossary of French Words

bonjour (bo-ZHOOR)   hello; good morning; good afternoon

bonsoir (bo-SWAH)   good evening

croissants (krwah-SAHNZ)   light, flaky, twisted bread rolls

Madame (mah-DAHM)   Mrs.; a married woman

Mademoiselle (mah-dah-mwah-ZEL)   Miss; an unmarried woman or girl

maman (muh-MAH)   mama

merci (mer-SEE)   thank you

Monsieur (mohn-SYUR)   Mr.; a man

ooh-la-la (OOH-lah-lah)   oh; wow

oui (wee)   yes

poupée (poo-PAY)   doll

voilà! (vwah-LAH)   There you have it! or There it is!

Questions and Answers About the 1890s

What happened to orphans in the 1890s?
In England, unwanted orphans and very poor, homeless people were often sent to workhouses. France did not have workhouses.

Workhouses were large buildings that looked like prisons. Adults and children who lived there wore uniforms, and their hair was cut short to help prevent lice. They were given small amounts of mush, bacon, cheese, bread, and potatoes to eat.

Everyone in the workhouse worked about ten hours a day. They were given hard or dull jobs in gardens, kitchens, or factories. Tasks included corn milling, sack making, and stone crushing. One of the most disliked jobs was rag picking (cutting pieces of old clothing apart to be sewn into new clothing).

Workhouses were overcrowded, and sickness spread easily. They were terrible places. People only went there if they had no other choice.

How were children treated in the 1890s?

In the 1890s, many people believed that children should be seen and not heard. That meant they were expected to be quiet, to use good manners, and not to bother adults.

Wealthy children were often raised by nannies. They spent most of their time in a nursery or playroom, away from their parents.

Girls and boys went to school, but most girls didn't learn subjects like math or history. They were taught things that would help them when they got married and had to run a household.

What did kids do for fun in the 1890s?

Children enjoyed simple games such as hopscotch, hoop and stick, and jackstraws.

To play hoop and stick, a child ran beside a large wooden hoop, hitting it with a stick to keep it rolling.

Jackstraws was a game similar to today's pickup sticks. A person would drop a bunch of thin sticks. Then they tried to remove one stick at a time without moving any of the other sticks.

Children and adults made animal shadow puppets on the wall for entertainment at home or at parties.

Some people made paper cutout silhouettes of the side view of a person's head. These silhouettes were framed and proudly displayed on parlor walls.

Popular books included *Alice's Adventures in Wonderland* by Lewis Carroll, *Black Beauty* by Anna Sewell, *The Adventures of Tom Sawyer* by Mark Twain, *The Merry Adventures of Robin Hood* by Howard Pyle, and *Heidi* by Johanna Spyri.

Watch for the sixth book in the
Doll Hospital™ series,
Charlotte's Choice,
coming soon.

♥

"Eenie, meanie, miney, moe," said Rose.

It was Saturday morning. She and Lila lay on the rug in the middle of their bedroom floor. They studied the Oak Hill Winter Carnival brochure spread out between them.

"There are too many things to choose from. I don't know what I'm going to do first," said Rose.

"I do." Lila pointed to a ride that looked like a big purple snowflake with spider legs. "I'm going on the Spinning Purple Snow Swirly." She looked at the brochure more closely. "Or maybe the Ice Scream Roller Coaster."

"You can't do two things first," said Rose.

"Why not?" asked Lila, trying to drive Rose crazy.

Rose leaned toward Lila and gave her The Eye. "I've decided on a ride. And I'm going to go on it right now. It's called the Screaming Purple Sister Stomper."

Lila laughed and scooted away before Rose could pounce. "Why don't you go on the Ice Scream Roser Toaster instead?"

"Shhh! Listen." Rose straightened and held up a hand for Lila to be quiet. They heard the click-clack sound of their grandmother's bead necklaces out in the hall. "Here comes Far Nana."

"Do you think she'll take us?" asked Lila.

Rose answered Lila in a voice loud enough for their grandmother to hear in the hall. "Far Nana is so-o-o nice. Of course she'll take us."

Far Nana smiled at them from the doorway. The smiley-face-snowman buttons on her sweater smiled at them, too. "Take you where?"

"Oh, hi, Far Nana." Rose pretended that she hadn't heard her grandmother coming from a mile away. "We have a great idea for our first day of winter vacation. We want to go to the Oak Hill Winter Carnival."

"You're going to lo-o-o-ve it," Lila promised.

They jumped up to show Far Nana the brochure.

"It does look like fun," Far Nana agreed.

"Yay!" said Lila.

"But I already made plans to take you girls to Mulberry Shaker Village," said Far Nana.

Lila slumped over. "Not yay."

"Where?" Rose asked in disbelief.

Far Nana looked from Rose to Lila and back. Her

smile faded, and she began twisting her bead necklaces. "Mulberry Shaker Village."

"Like saltshakers? A whole village of them?" asked Lila.

"No. Shakers were people who lived together like a big family," Far Nana explained. "They built the village more than two hundred years ago. Now tourists can visit it to see how the Shakers once lived."

"But we could go there anytime," said Rose.

Far Nana shook her head no. "I promised an old friend of mine who works at the village that we'd come. She asked me to repair a Shaker doll while we visit."

"What about the Oak Hill Winter Carnival?" asked Rose.

"You can go another time," said Far Nana.

"No, we can't. It's full of ice and snow. It'll all melt pretty soon," said Rose.

"And this week is a once-in-a-wintertime event. It says so right here." Lila held the brochure closer to Far Nana's glasses to be sure she could read the big purple letters. They said:

COME TO OAK HILL WINTER CARNIVAL'S
ONCE-IN-A-WINTERTIME EVENT!
SPECIAL RIDES AND ACTIVITIES
FOR KIDS ON
WINTER BREAK

Far Nana sighed. "I wish you'd said something sooner."

"Why didn't you say something sooner about the Shaker place?" asked Lila.

"I wanted it to be a surprise," their grandmother explained.

"It is," grumbled Rose. "The yucky kind."

Rose and Lila tried to think of reasons why they couldn't go.

Rose came up with one. "Mom and Dad won't know where to call us."

"And what about the cats?" asked Lila.

"I'll give your parents the village's phone number so they can call you there if anything important comes up," said Far Nana. "And I'll ask your friend Nadia from next door to take care of the cats while we're gone."

"But we told the other kids at school we were going to the Winter Carnival," said Lila. "We can't be the only ones who don't show up!"

Far Nana folded her arms like she meant business. "I'm sorry, but I've made my decision. So let's get packing. It's a three-hour drive." She turned and left their bedroom.

Rose flopped on her bed. "When I grow up, I'm going to let my grandkids do what they want on winter vacation. She's not being fair."

"No-Fair-Far-Nana. That's her new name," said Lila.

"But we have to follow Far Nana's rules," Rose pointed out. "Mom and Dad said."

"Mom and Dad!" said Lila. "Great idea. Let's call them. Maybe they can change Far Nana's mind."

Rose sat up. "We're only supposed to call them for emergencies."

"This *is* an emergency," said Lila. "Let's go."

While Far Nana was in her room packing, Rose and Lila tiptoed downstairs. They dialed their mom and dad's phone number in Africa.

The girls held the phone between them, so they could both hear. They listened to their mom's voice on the answering machine. As usual, they had to leave voice mail. Their parents were always busy working in the African villages.

After the beep, Rose's words tumbled out fast. "Mom, Far Nana is being mean."

"She's making us go to the saltshaker village for winter vacation," Lila butted in.

"But we want to go to the Oak Hill Winter Carnival," said Rose. "Make her stop bossing us around, okay?"

"Yeah. She's ruining our vacation," said Lila.

They were quiet for a second, listening to long-distance air.

Rose wound her fingers in the curls of the phone cord. "I wish you would come home. I miss you."

"Yeah," said Lila. "Ditto."

Joan Holub

About the Author

When Joan Holub was a girl, her best friend, Ann, lived right down the street. Ann had lots of toys. But she had one special doll that Joan loved best — a beautiful ballerina. It had lace-up shoes and a frilly satin tutu. Its body was jointed and bendable.

After a few years, Joan's family moved away. Ann gave the doll to Joan as a going-away present. Joan named the doll Annie, after her friend. She made lots of clothes for Annie, using her mother's sewing machine.

Joan played with Annie so much that she wore her out. Annie's arms and legs came apart. She needed help! So Joan and her mother took Annie to a doll hospital. There, Annie's arms and legs were put back together. She even got a new wig.

Annie and some of her doll friends still live in Washington State with Joan, her husband, George, and their two cats.

Joan Holub is the author and/or illustrator of many books for children. You can find out more about Joan and her books on her Web site, *www.joanholub.com.*